For J.C., with hopes of inspiring a more loving, compassionate world for children everywhere—K.B.
For Margot, who I'm wild about—J.S.

Houghton Mifflin Harcourt
Boston   New York

WILD About US!

Written by **Karen Beaumont**

Illustrated by **Janet Stevens**

I'M WARTY WARTHOG!

Can't be who I'm not.

I am who I am,

and I've got what I've got.

I have **TUSKS**! I have **WARTS**!

But I like what I see!

In my own special way,

I'm as cute as can be.

YESSIRREE!

We all are the way

we are all meant to be!

Crocodile's proud

of his big

toothy grin.

Rhino feels fine in her . . .

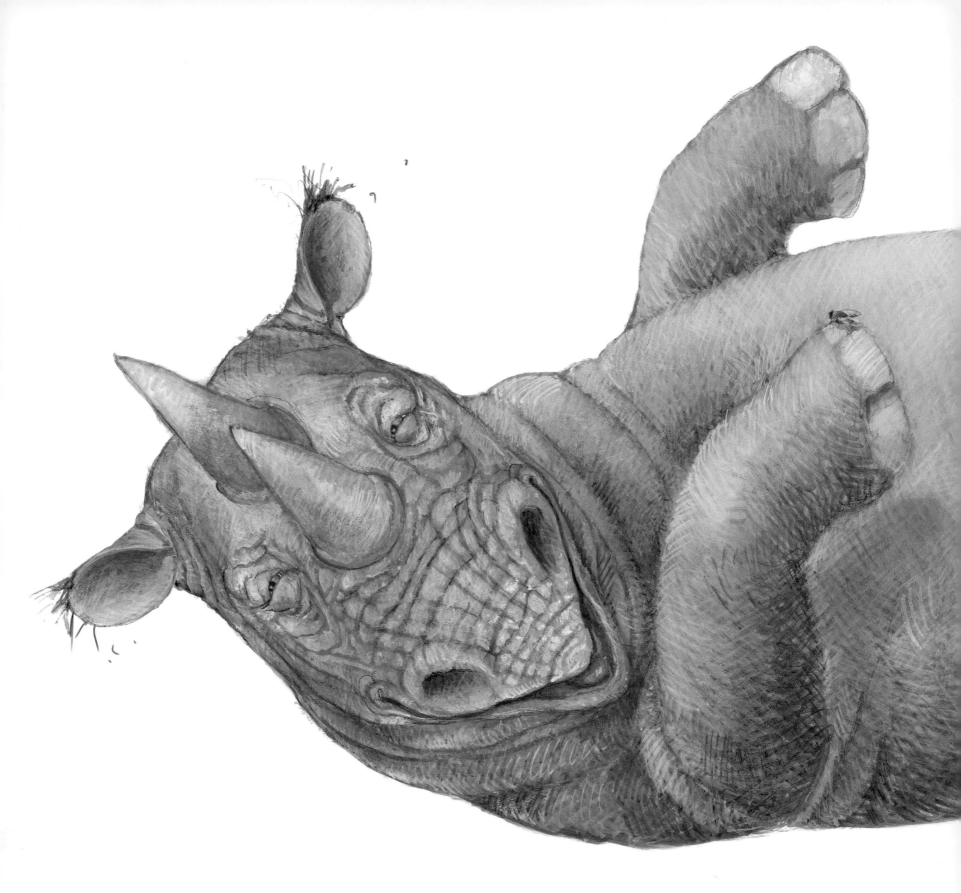

wrinkly skin.

Elephant's confident nothing is wrong.

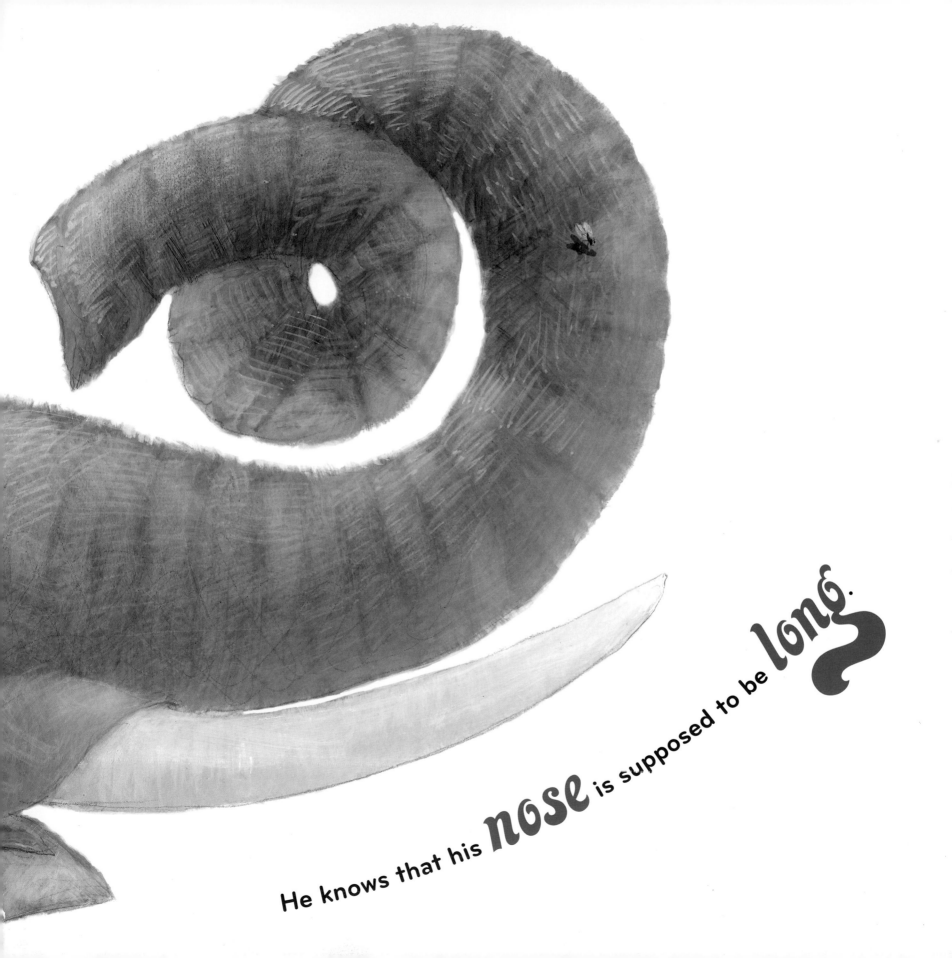

He knows that his **nose** is supposed to be **long**.

No one laughs at Giraffe 'cause she's LANKY and TALL.

Here at the zoo,

there is room for us all.

Would you dare tell Flamingo

he shouldn't be pink?

Or Potbellied Pig she's too

plump, do you think?

We never tease Tortoise for being so slow.

He's . . . not . . . meant . . . to . . . hurry . . .

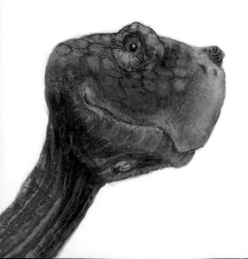

or . . . scurry, . . . you . . . know.

Does Porcupine care that she can't *curl* her *hair*?

Is Leopard upset he has . . .

SPOTS

everywhere?

Hippo is happy!

She loves her behind!

It wiggles!
It jiggles!

It's one-of-a-kind!

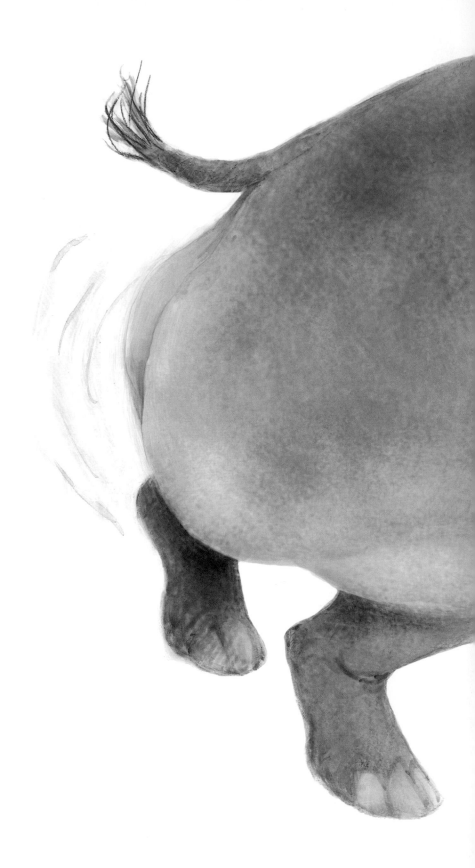

She's proud of precisely

the way it's designed.

Chimp's **ears** stick out,

as you clearly can see . . .

But he thinks they're charming,
and we all agree!

Kangaroo has

HUGE FEET,

but you don't see her pout.

She has much better things

to be thinking about!

We're glad we're all different!

It would be such a shame

if you came to the zoo . . .

and we all looked the same!